DISCARDED

D1275161

L 3872

THE CIRCUS
AND OTHER STORIES

FOUR BOOKS BY
SAMUIL MARSHAK &
VLADIMIR LEBEDEV

TRANSLATED BY STEPHEN CAPUS

WITH AN AFTERWORD BY OLGA MÄEOTS

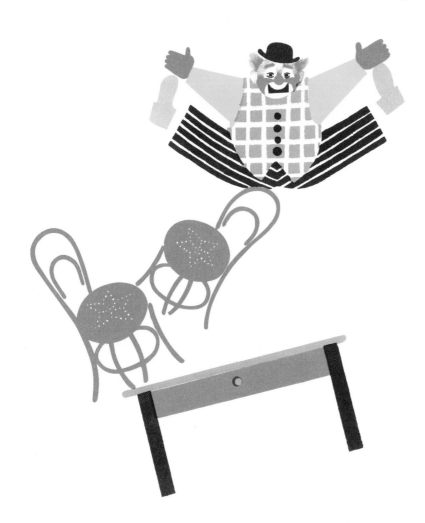

TATE PUBLISHING

THE CIRCUS

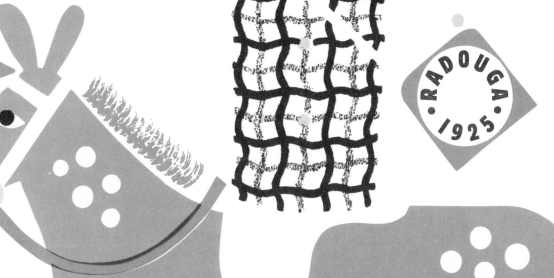

RADOUGA · 1925 ·

S. MARSHAK
V. LEBEDEV

FOR THE TIME **FIRST IN RUSSIA**

!! !!

THE CIRCUS

For the first time in Russia
We present with great pleasure
The famed Tsaniboni's
Circus: trained ponies,
Donkeys, bright lights
And all manner of sights
For your general delight!

A rider from Rio,
An aerial trio,
The wrestler Ivan
Who's so strong that he can
Overcome his opponent
In just a few moments
— Whoever the man!

Jacko, the famous clown
Who's just arrived in town
All the way from Paris.
He always looks so harassed,
Dishevelled and embarrassed,
For every hour, perhaps,
He receives a thousand slaps.

Splendid displays!
So little to pay!
Full houses each evening! Stormy applause!
The stalls — fifty copecks, a box — rather more.
And when, at the end
There's no more to see,
We'll let you go home for free!

THIS MAN, LIKE A BIRD ON THE TOP OF A TREE

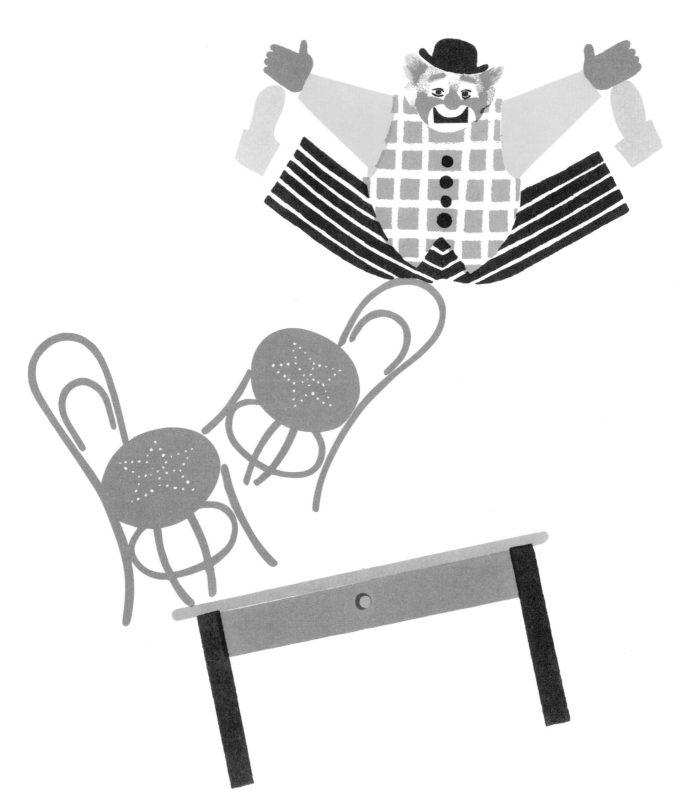

CAN PERCH ON THE SPIRE OF THE ADMIRALTY!

JUGGLING ABOVE HIS HEAD LIKE SKITTLES
A VASE, A BOTTLE AND A LITTLE

CHILD, HE THROWS THEM UP IN THE AIR,
THEN CATCHES THEM WITHOUT A CARE.

ACCOMPANIED BY DRUMS, THE CRACK AND WHISTLE OF THE WHIP,

DON PEDRO ON A HORSE'S BACK PERFORMS HIS DARING TRICKS.

MADEMOISELLE FRICASSÉ

UPON ONE WHEEL RIDES BY —
AND THEN SHE'S GONE.

ALONG THE WIRE A LADY GOES.

A TELEPHONE CALL PROCEEDS JUST SO.

SO WELL DOES JUMBO PLAY THE DRUMS
THAT ALL THE PIONEERS SAY

THEY WISH THAT JUMBO COULD BECOME
A MEMBER OF THEIR TEAM ONE DAY.

EXCUSE ME, SIR, WHERE DID YOU FIND A RED TOMATO OF THAT KIND?

YOU'RE VERY RUDE, I'LL HAVE YOU KNOW: THAT'S NO TOMATO – THAT'S MY NOSE!

THESE MEN OF STRENGTH BEYOND COMPARE
CAN TOSS THEIR WEIGHTS UP IN THE AIR

AND INTERCEPT THEM WHEN THEY FALL
AS CHILDREN CATCH A BOUNCING BALL.

FISHING IN THE ORCHESTRA
JUST NOW, BY CHANCE I HOOKED

THIS LITTLE CARP. WHEN I GO HOME
TONIGHT, I'LL HAVE IT COOKED.

SPIRIDON KUZMICH, THE FAMOUS CLOWN,
IS A NATIVE SON OF MOSCOW TOWN.

BUT DARYA, HIS WIFE, IS WITH US TODAY
FROM A FOREIGN LAND THAT'S FAR AWAY.

I'M MISS JENNY, SWEET AND BLONDE,
I PRANCE AROUND THE RING UPON

A CRIMSON SADDLE EVERY DAY:
GEE UP! GEE UP! LET'S GO! ALLEZ!

ИЗДАТЕЛЬСТВО РАДУГА

S.MARSHAK

ICE CREAM

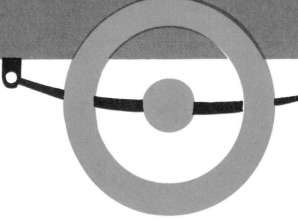

V. LEBEDEV

DRAWINGS

RADOUGA
1925

A painted hand-cart rolls
Clattering along the road;
As he drives the cart about
An old man begins to shout:

"Ice cream,
Strawberry,
Peppermint,
Lime,
Step this way and stand in line!"

And the bare foot children start
To follow the little cart.
And when at last it stops,
All around the children flock.

And the ice cream, so sweet,
Is ladled upon
Little dishes. Now eat
It all up, till it's gone!

To the cart a fat man runs,
Perspiring in the sun.
On his head he wears a hat
And his cheeks are round and fat.

And he shouts out as he runs:
"One ice cream, please, old man!"

So the old man takes a spoon,
And he takes a wafer, too;
He dips the spoon in the tub
And scoops the ice cream up.
Then, smoothing the ice cream flat,
Puts a wafer on top of that.

"Here's one pound fifty more —
No, make that three pounds, for
It so happens that today's
My birthday", the fat man says.
"If that's what you prefer,
I'm at your service sir!"

And the fat man eats it up.
He doesn't waste a drop.
    But the people fear the worst:
They're sure he's going to burst!
And now here he is again:
First he spends a fiver, then

Ten more, as the crowd all shout:
"Oh, fat man, please watch out!
Your head has turned quite blue
And there's frost on your whiskers, too,
And, suspended from the tip
Of your nose, an icicle drips!"

And as for the ice cream — it
Has vanished, every bit.

Clattering along the road,
An empty hand-cart rolls,
The old man who drives it sends
This greeting to his friends:

"Hey there, colleagues, say
What's business like today?
A fat man's bought my stock
And he's gobbled up the lot!"

And his friends with merry hearts
Push their heavy carts,
And, gathering in a crowd,
Proclaim their wares out loud:

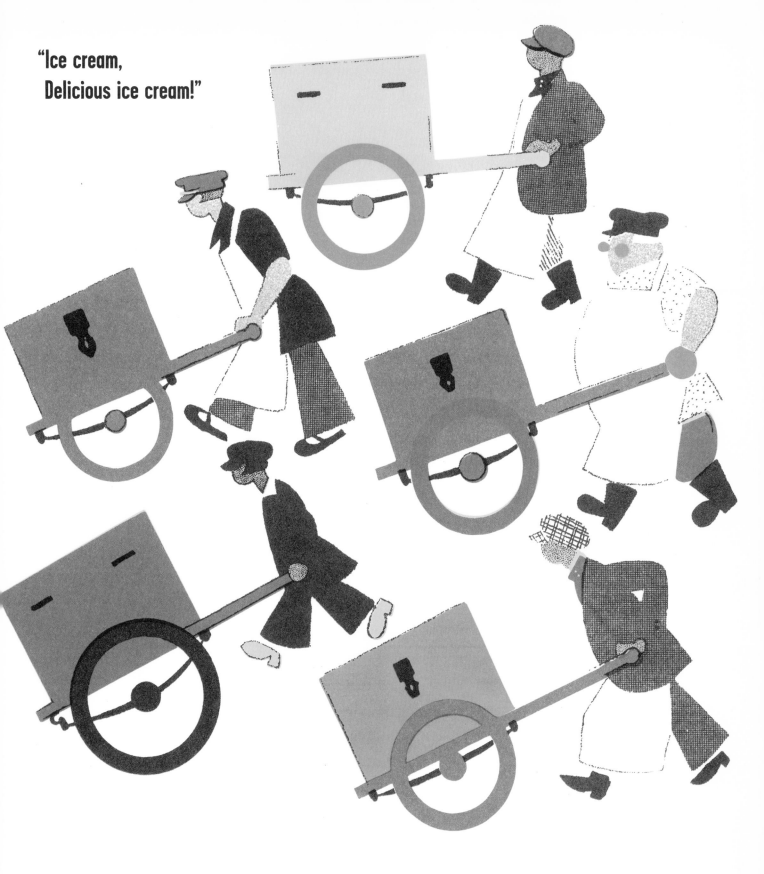

"Ice cream,
Delicious ice cream!"

"Pineapple,
Strawberry,

Apple,
Pear ...

Get your birthday
Ice cream here!"

But the fat man's still not done,
No, he's only just begun.

For he grabs an entire pot
And swallows down the lot

And by now the hand which holds
His wallet is icy cold.

There's a snow drift on his shoulders
And his forehead's frozen over,
Frost on his glasses glisters,
And there's ice on his frozen whiskers.

And he stands there without stirring,
All around a blizzard whirling!

Oh, what a wonderful sight!
A snow-drift overnight,
Four foot deep,
Has covered our street
To the children's huge delight!

Fetch your skates without delay,
Hurry and find your sleigh!
Summer is here,
The streets are all clear,
But we'll play in the snow all day!

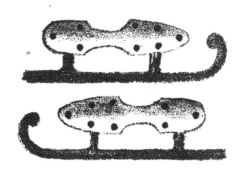

YESTERDAY

S. *Marshak* AND V. *Lebedev*

TODAY

RADOUGA   1925

A KEROSENE LAMP,
A CANDLE OF WAX,

A YOKE WITH A BUCKET,
AN INK-WELL AND PEN.

Behind some firewood, out of sight,
A kerosene lamp bewailed her plight:

        I'm hungry,
        I'm cold,
My shade is thick with dust,
My wick is all dried up.
        The reason why
        No one needs me, I
Can't explain, however I try.

But when they used to light me
Each night, the moths all came
Fluttering through the window
To perish in my flame.
And I looked on with indifference
Through my sombre smoked glass shade
As an ancient copper kettle
Whistled by my side.

In the canteen as I ate
My lunch today I met
A lamp in which, they say,
Fifty candles blaze away.

You're joking! Do you call
That a lamp? It's just a ball
Of glass, inside which there
Are two or three small hairs.

"Madam" – I said – "I doubt
That you come from hereabouts.
So I'd be curious to learn
Precisely how you burn.
For who could ever light
A lamp that's sealed so tight?"

"But what's it got to do" –
The stranger replied – "with you?"

Of course, I bridled at
A reply as rude as that.
"In this house for ten years I've
Lighted up the people's lives,
Nor once smoked in all that time.
And it's no affair of mine?"

"And" – I add – "on top of this
I need no clever tricks
To burn, no strange devices,
For me a match suffices –
I burn as candles do.
But who could light up you?
        You're a fraud,
        You're not a
Lamp, you're an imposter!"

And she replied to me:

"You're really rather simple:
As anyone can see,
    Your wick burns much too dimly,
But, in the meantime, I
    Dispense illumination
Like the lightening in the sky
    Who's my very close relation!"

I'M AN ELEC TRICAL ECO NOMICAL LAMP!

"I've no need of kerosene.
From the station a machine
Sends a current down the wire.
I'm not just any kind of phial!"

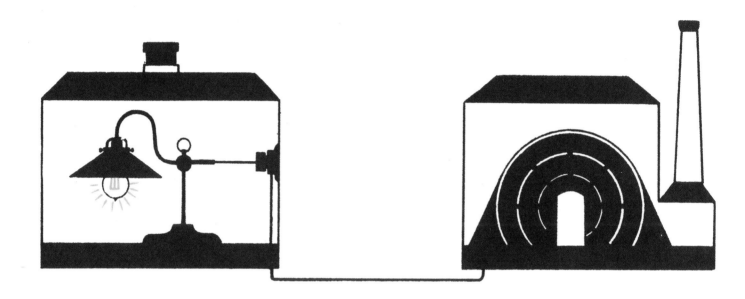

"Each time the switch unites
Two filaments, my light
Begins to brightly glow.
Have you understood by now?"

THE CANDLE WITH TREPIDATION

MAKES THIS OBSERVATION:

"IN THE LIGHT BULB, SO YOU SAY,

FIFTY CANDLES BURN AWAY.

BUT THEY'VE FOOLED YOU — FOR INSIDE

NOT ONE CANDLE CAN BE SPIED!"

A pen began to speak
From an empty pot of ink:
"The ink I used to sup
From the ink well's all dried up.

I'm surplus to requirements,
I'm living in retirement.
I've turned to rust and in
My ink small insects swim.

Our owner now resorts
To pens of other sorts.
They thunder, every one,
Like a battery of guns."

"The little hammers

Time after time

Beat out commas,

Full-stops,

Lines.

Half the machine sits tight,

The other moves to the right...

Why does it act this way?

I can't begin to say!"

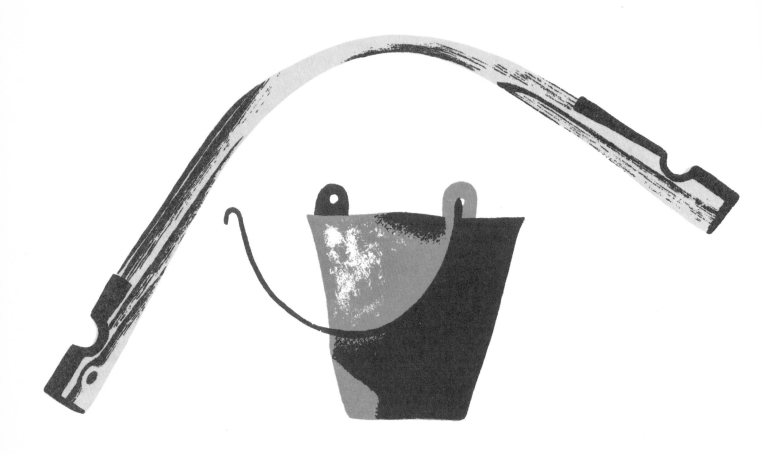

A yoke and a bucket
Kick up a racket:

With a bucket who goes running
For water any more?
Since they installed the plumbing
Life's different from before.

Have all the wives and daughters
Lately grown soft and weak?
The river now brings the water
The girls once went to seek.

But once the women would go
To the river and kneel down low,
And as they set off to bring
The water, they used to sing.

They used to go to the river
And bow to her with respect.
"Greetings, mother, please give us
Some water to collect."

But today fresh water can
Belong to anyone –
You simply turn your hand,
The water starts to run!

Life today is quite devoid
Of sense – and yokes are unemployed...

ИЗДАТЕЛЬСТВО РАДУГА

S. MARSHAK · V. LEBEDEV

HOW THE PLANE MADE A PLANE

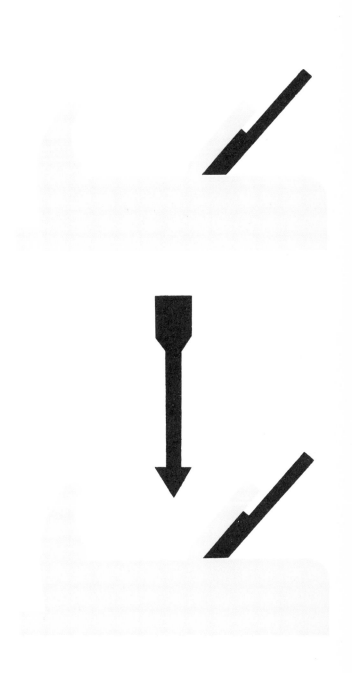

STORY · RADOUGA · 1927 · LENINGRAD

Early one day
As he laboured away
    At his chores an old plane
    Began to complain:

"You old fool, what's the good
Of scraping this wood!
You no longer obtain
A smooth shave when you plane.
But there once was a time
When you planed and a fine
White ribbon of wood
Curled up as it should ...
You once were a true
Old plane: thanks to you
Many planks in the past
Have been shaped. But at last,
Having lost your good health,
You must lie on the shelf."

"What causes you grizzle
 In this manner?" asked the chisel.

With a crash the mallet added:
"When you're gone, how will we manage?"

"And who can take your place
 If you leave us?" squeaked the brace.

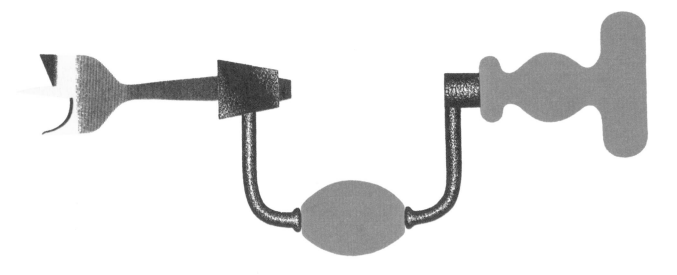

"We'll certainly all miss you!"
The slender tooth plane whispered.

And the workbench croaked: "It's true:
Without you what will we do?"

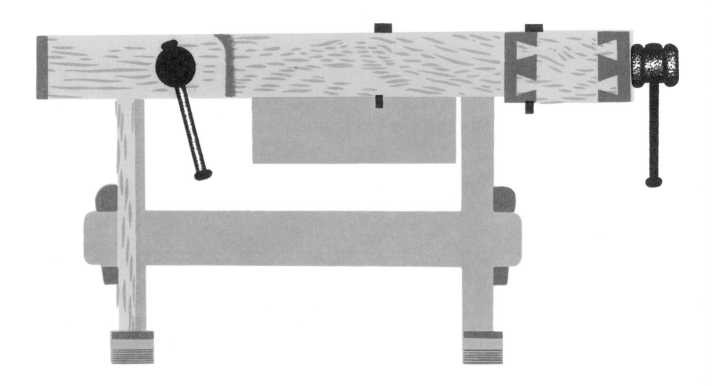

"What's the point of all this strife?"
The plane asked. "All my life
I've laboured – now I'm tired
And it's time that I retired.
But before I can escape
I need an heir to take my place.

And so my sister, saw, I ask
That you should carry out this task:
In the wood please find a tree
From which to make a plane like me."

And the saw replied: "OK"
And wriggled on her way.

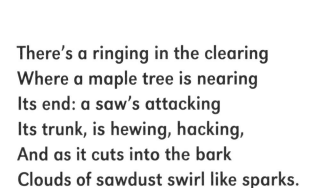

There's a ringing in the clearing
Where a maple tree is nearing
Its end: a saw's attacking
Its trunk, is hewing, hacking,
And as it cuts into the bark
Clouds of sawdust swirl like sparks.

Then, emitting one last groan,
The tree comes crashing down,
Till it hits the ground below
And sinks into the snow.

Oh, maple, your skin
Has been tempered in
The frost and the sun.
That's why you're the one
For us – you'll look so good
When you're trimmed from head to foot!

And the saw rode away
From the wood on a sleigh.
"Hey, I've brought a maple tree
For your replacement – come and see!"

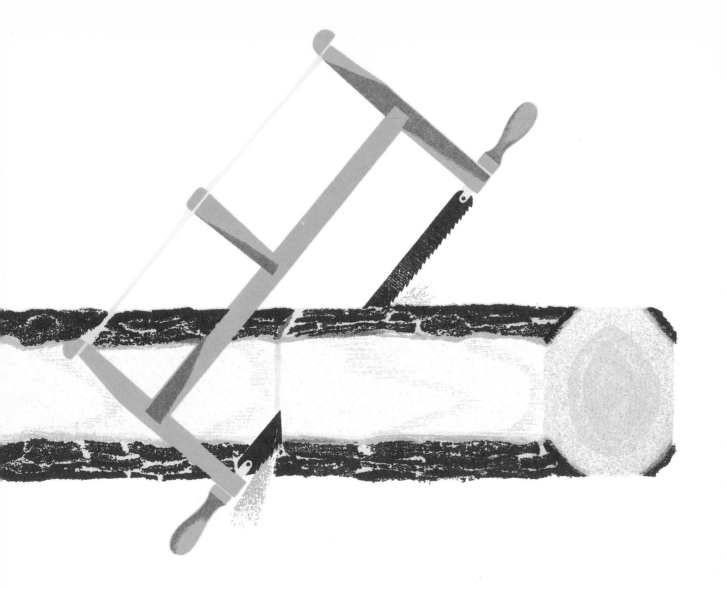

And the plane exclaimed: "That's it!
Now cut it into bits!"

And they gripped it like a vice,
And they sawed it, slice by slice.

And the plane said: "As you know,
I need an heir before I go.
What I want is one who's not
All twisted into knots,
Who isn't full of mould,
Who will serve to reach our goal!"

Here's a lovely little block:
There's the base and here's the top.
We'll add a handle at the tip,
After that a metal bit,
Then we'll knock a slender wedge in
And round off all the edges.

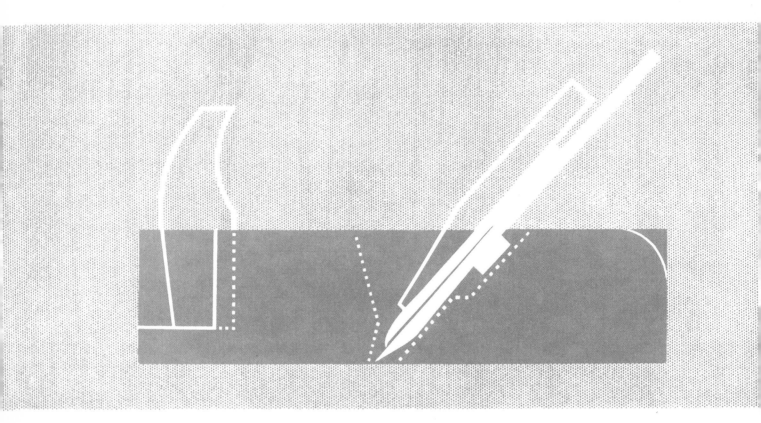

And now, my child,
Lie on your side,

While I trim your border
And put it in order.

And when that side's done
We'll do the other one.

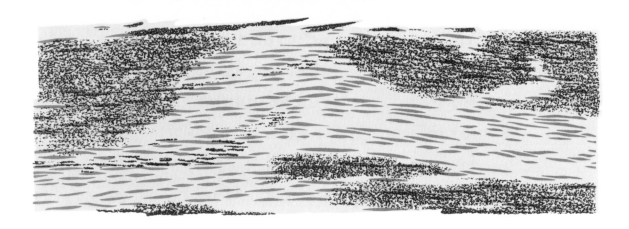

You're rough and you're covered
In smudges all over.

And so let's make a start
Till we've cleaned every part!

I'll work you every way
Till I've shaved the bumps away.
One more time until at last
You'll gleam as smooth as glass!

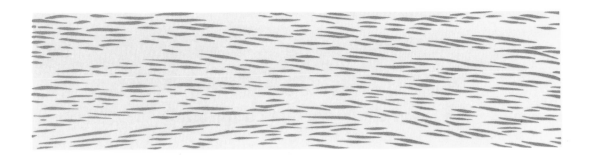

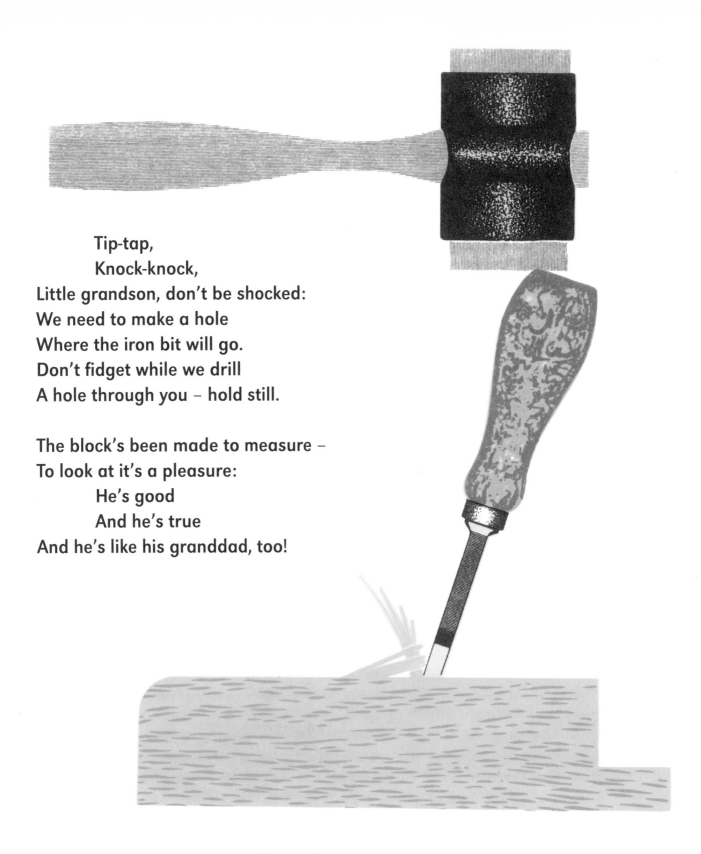

Tip-tap,
Knock-knock,
Little grandson, don't be shocked:
We need to make a hole
Where the iron bit will go.
Don't fidget while we drill
A hole through you – hold still.

The block's been made to measure –
To look at it's a pleasure:
He's good
And he's true
And he's like his granddad, too!

He's a handsome grandson, but
Still he lacks a tooth which cuts.

"Dear hammer, be so kind
As to tap on my behind,
Shake my body, mallet,
Till you've opened wide my gullet
And my little iron tooth
And my maple tongue come loose."

"My grandson, now you
Will have a tooth, too!"

"And now, my little one,
There's work which must be done,
That beech plank over there
Waits to be prepared.
   Then work with a will,
    Go at it until
The shavings and the curls
Of wood begin to whirl."

ИЗДАТЕЛЬСТВО РАДУГА

TRANSLATOR'S NOTE

Samuil Marshak was born in Vornezh in 1887, where his father worked as a factory foreman. He showed promise of literary talent at an early age, producing a translation of a poem by Horace when he was eleven. After his family moved to Saint Petersburg in 1902 he was introduced to Maxim Gorky, who remained a supporter and friend until he died in 1936.

From 1912 to 1914 Marshak studied at the University of London. During his stay in England he acquired a thorough knowledge of the English language and read widely in English poetry. After the death of his daughter in 1915 he also began to take an interest in English nursery rhymes. It was at this time, too, that he produced his first translations from English poetry, including versions of the poems of William Blake.

In 1923 Marshak published his first poems for children with the publishing house Radouga. In 1925, he became head of the children's section at the Leningrad State Publishing House, and later, at the instigation of Gorky, he helped to set up the children's publisher Detgiz.

Having spent the period of the Second World War serving as a publicist, producing anti-Nazi satires, as well as working on translations of the poems of Robert Burns and Shakespeare's sonnets, he devoted most of his final decade, following the death of Stalin, to writing original lyric poetry. He died in 1964.

Samuil Marshak's poems for children are written in a verse which displays a high degree of prosodic formality. His rhymes and rhythms make an important contribution to the distinctive character of his compositions, to which they impart a quality which is often reminiscent of Russian folk poetry.

It is for this reason – as well as the fact that children tend to be highly conservative in matters of prosody – that the translator of Marshak's verse for children cannot have recourse to the usual solution to the problem of translating foreign verse forms into English – which is to ignore them altogether and concentrate instead on the content. The translator of Marshak's poems, then, has no choice but to look for a way to transpose his evocative rhythms and rhymes into English verse. Fortunately, a model for this difficult art has been provided by Samuil Marshak himself, who in his translations of English poetry produced formally accomplished versions of poets such as Shakespeare, Robert Burns and William Blake which quickly became a much loved part of the Russian poetic repertoire. I hope that the translations in this volume will represent a small gesture toward repaying the debt owed to Samuil Marshak by English poetry.

Stephen Capus

AFTERWORD

Russian art in 1920s – the first decade after the Revolution – is well known for its achievements in avant-garde. Seen mainly as experiments in painting, sculpture and architecture, the innovations in book art are much less familiar. However, book art is an area where the connection between revolutionary enthusiasm, faith in a communist utopia of a new world and revolutionary art experimentation is most obvious, especially with children's books.

The 1920s are considered to be a golden age in the history of Russian children's books. The task set by the Soviet government to bring books to the new generation of 'young constructors of communism' inspired many talented artists and authors, who wished to contribute to the upbringing of 'a new society' and considered it a unique chance that gave infinite possibilities for creative experimentation. The role of children's books as an effective educational tool was reconsidered. The small world of the old nursery opened up to the boundless panorama of reality. Children's books explored new themes and images, and new language and rhythms.

The leading figures of this movement were the artist Vladimir Lebedev (1891–1967) and the poet Samuil Marshak (1887–1964). They not only created children's books that still impress with their daring novelty but they also expanded the boundaries of book art. They founded a school of artists and writers – known as the Leningrad School – who boldly experimented with form and style as well as with themes and ideas for the books; together they set the highest standards in art for children.

Both Lebedev and Marshak drew on their previous creative experience in children's books. In Lebedev's case this included his thorough study of drawing from nature, his interest in Russian folk graphics, known as 'lubok', his work on political posters for the information agency ROSTA Windows and his interest in European impressionist and cubist painting. All these influences had been never accepted automatically but contributed to the creation of a unique personal style marked by the highest professionalism and interest in human nature as opposed to the abstract experiments of many artists of the time. Lebedev was an outstanding artist open to bold experimentation, which all too often aroused criticism and caused difficulties but nevertheless ensured him a leading position in many fields of art.

Samuil Marshak became interested in children's literature relatively early. He was inspired by Russian children's lore, and, when studying in London in 1912–14, the young poet became fascinated by English nursery rhymes, many of which he later translated into Russian. He praised these amusing verses for their vividness, lack of sentimentality and variety of dynamic rhythms. Marshak wished to rid children's books of superfluous sentimentality, pedagogical didacticism and ideological dogma; instead he wanted them to be windows opening on to a real world full of miracles of its own.

In the 1920s Lebedev and Marshak worked in the publishing house Radouga (Rainbow) in Leningrad where a striving for perfection was the main impulse for creating children's books and luckily more important than conforming to ideological demands. The books included in this edition belong to that most prolific period in their careers.

The Circus presents the first example of a collaboration between Lebedev and Marshak. It was also the first time both the author and the illustrator were published together on the front cover, showing they were equally important. Pictures that look very much like circus posters appeared first and the text was written afterwards, but together they create a dynamic unity. Lebedev proved his ideas on book design with this title where all elements contributed to the whole and a book was not just decorated but constructed like a building.

The book is staged as a circus performance: each page revealing a new act. The characters almost lack individual features. They look like theatre masks presenting various circus genres – clowns, acrobats and jugglers. Their bright and eccentric appearance attracts children and introduces them to the circus world. While Lebedev did not imitate children's drawings, he manages to come near to a child's way of perception. The figures are put on a blank background, which makes them more intense and provokes the readers' imagination to start playing with them as children play with toys, creating imaginary worlds of their own and supplying dolls with the personal characteristics required for a play.

In *Ice Cream* the verse was written first. A variety of rhythms – playful and imitating the street chorus – vivid fantasy and a good dollop of nonsense make this poem lively and modern. The amusing incident involves not only a greedy person but a bourgeois, a representative of the condemned class, borrowing from the trend in political caricatures of the time. But the unlucky hero is depicted with sympathy rather than satire; he looks funny but not unattractive.

Here again Lebedev avoids linear drawings and prefers combinations of coloured dots that create various textures. The images seem to be very simple, but while laconic, they are highly expressive and dynamic. The lack of background does not deprive the book of scenery: we can imagine the busy street life on a hot sunny day, and even hear the clamour of the city.

Samuil Marshak

В.В.Лебедев
V.V.Lebedev
W.W.Lebedev
1928

Vladimir Lebedev, 1928

Yesterday and Today is a story about the most important changes in everyday life that children would have witnessed at that time. The confrontation between past and present (and the victory of the later) is revealed to children in the form of a tale. Lebedev tried to avoid didacticism, preferring to show rather than explain: the world of today is full of dynamic, joyful rhythms and bright colours. Its images are clear and concrete. On the contrary, the world of yesterday is vague and decrepit – its objects are as crooked as old people. Look at the candlestick! The book is a masterpiece of design; its layout presents the perfect unity of various elements: pictures, fragments of text and a variety of typefaces. Lebedev makes typography work as a visual object. He chooses a specific typographical look to illustrate the meaning: the page with handwriting written with an old pen is covered with ugly ink spots, while the opposite page shows a typewriter and the text here is neat and clear. The new technical world is presented to a child as attractive and challenging.

Although the industrial book was a popular genre of new Soviet children's literature, Marshak and Lebedev did not follow an official pattern in *How the Plane Made a Plane*. They address their book to very small children, not in a non-fictional book but as a tale. The goal was not only to introduce a child to a profession but to make it look attractive. They wanted to show the traditions of the trade, the beauty of labour, its creative force and, last but not least, turn this experience into a play. The artist shows simple tools in a very matter-of-fact way: the drawings look like they are from a professional manual or a design for tools, but at the same time they seem alive – as they should in a tale!

Vladimir Lebedev and Samuil Marshak collaborated on approximately fifty titles, which were published and republished in dozens of editions. For every new edition Lebedev made new illustrations – thus each book marked a new stage in his creative development. But it is his earliest books from the 1920s that remain second to none. The increased ideological pressure from the mid-1930s ended any experimentation in art and established the yoke of socialist realism. Never again in his long life, after that happy decade full of free creative spirit, did Vladimir Lebedev have the opportunity to express himself to the utmost of his talent. The artist was aware of this and said 'I'm an artist of the 1920s – there lies the key to all my art'.

For those book lovers who have had a chance to admire these masterpieces, they still remain avant-garde and seem to belong to an optimistic future rather than a vintage past.

Olga Mäeots
M.I. Rudomino All-Russia State Library for Foreign Literature, Moscow

Marshak, S. (Samuil), 1887-1964,
author
The circus and other stories
33500011621877 ldn

First published 2013 by order of
the Tate Trustees by Tate Publishing,
a division of Tate Enterprises Ltd,
Millbank, London SW1P 4RG
www.tate.org.uk/publishing

This edition © Tate 2013

First published in French as *Collection des Trois Ourses*,
Editions MeMo, Nantes 2005 © Editions MeMo, 2005
Text © The Estate Samuil Marshak 2013
Images © The Estate of Vladimir Lebedev 2013
Translation © Tate 2013

All rights reserved. No part of this book may be reprinted or reproduced or utilised
in any form or by any electronic, mechanical or other means, now known or hereafter
invented, including photocopying and recording, or in any information storage or
retrieval system, without permission in writing from the publishers or a licence from
the Copyright Licensing Agency Ltd, www.cla.co.uk

A catalogue record for this book is available from the British Library
ISBN 978-1-84976-102-4

Distributed in the United States and Canada by ABRAMS, New York
Library of Congress Control Number applied for

Colour reproduction by Evergreen Colour Separation Co. Ltd, Hong Kong
Printed in China by Toppan Leefung Printing Ltd